Mariella Can't Wait

By Madelyn Grace Modeste

© Madelyn Grace Modeste 2020
Illustrations by Jennifer Linda
All rights reserved.

This book is a product of Jacky Lamenzo's Writing and Publishing class.

www.jackylamenzo.com

I dedicate this book to my mom Shauntelle and dad Philbert who love me so much. They encouraged me to write this first book and work hard on it. I also dedicate this book to my Grandmother Joyce who cares about me so much. She sends me sweet gifts and surprises all of the time from Arkansas.

Mariella is a 10 year old girl. She lives with her loving family and cat Thelma.

She's excited about a very special package from her grandmother from out of state.

Mariella can't wait.

Her mom told her that she would be receiving a special gift from her grandmother.

Mariella expected it to arrive in three days since it was coming from a nearby state and normally mail does not take long to arrive from there.

She can't wait.

Mariella kept asking her mom about the special package every day.

Her mom told her to be patient. Mariella became impatient.

She can't wait.

Mariella tried to keep her mind off the package by playing with her cat, Thelma. This didn't work.

She always loved playing with her cat, but she can't wait.

A week had passed, and Mariella continued to check her mailbox every day.

So she decided to watch her favorite baking show with her mom.

Mariella started baking her own favorite red velvet cupcakes. This wasn't a great distraction, either.

She could not wait.

Mariella was becoming really frustrated.

Now her mom decided to check with Mariella's grandmother.

Her mother called Mariella's grandmother again.

She found out it was a problem with the special package that made the delivery process longer than usual.

Mariella felt a little bit better.

But still, she can't wait.

Finally Mariella decided to just keep moving on with all of the fun things she normally did with her family.

Mariella went to the local park and played soccer with her family.

Two long weeks later the special package arrived!

Mariella learned a valuable lesson on how to be patient. She realized that she was not able to control things that were uncontrollable.

She called her grandmother, thanked her and told her she loved her.

Mariella finally received her hot pink facemask that she is proud to wear out in public!

It was the best gift ever and worth the wait.

Made in the USA
Coppell, TX
06 October 2025